RABINDRANATH TAGORE

two sisters

Translated from the Bengali original with an Introduction by

Nirmal Kanti Bhattacharjee

THORNBIRD
NIYOGI BOOKS

Published by
NIYOGI BOOKS
Block D, Building No. 77,
Okhla Industrial Area, Phase-I,
New Delhi-110 020, INDIA
Tel: 91-11-26816301, 26818960
Email: niyogibooks@gmail.com
Website: www.niyogibooksindia.com

Editor: Mohua Mitra
Design: Shashi Bhushan Prasad

ISBN: 978-93-86906-66-3
Publication: 2018

Printed at: Niyogi Offset Pvt. Ltd., New Delhi, India

INTRODUCTION

If the manuscripts of *Dui Bon* (Two Sisters) preserved in the Rabindra Bhavan archive at Santiniketan are carefully scrutinised, one will realise that though Rabindranath made quite a few drafts of the novelette, he did not mention the date of composition anywhere. From the circumstantial evidences like a reference in the *Rabindrajiboni* by Prabhat Kumar Mukhopadhyay or in a letter written by Tagore to Nirmalkumari Mahalanobis, one can only assume that he prepared the first draft of the novelette by 23 October, 1932. It was first serialised in four consecutive issues of the magazine *Bichitra*, beginning from November, 1932 and was published in book form by March, 1933.

Like John Donnes' poetry, *Two Sisters* is a book of 'fine onset'. At the very beginning, Tagore comes out with a statement about feminine nature and it seems the entire narrative is the fictionalisation of that idea. The first sentence of the novel says, 'Women are of two types; that is what I have heard from some scholars. One is of mother category, the other is of lover' and the story goes on to establish Sharmila and her sister Urmimala as the embodiments of these two types. However, for full blossoming of their characters they need a peg and Sharmila's husband, Shashanka serves the purpose of that peg. The devoted husband and the successful businessman suddenly discovered his romantic side, coming in contact with the sprightly and playful Urmimala. Here Tagore does not fail to offer an antithesis of sorts in Nirod, the grim and presumptuous fiance of Urmimala. The authorial sympathy, however, seems to be with Sharmila, the propitious housewife, soft and affectionate, ready to take all the burden of her husband on her slender shoulders. The conflict in the story was resolved by Sharmila's miraculous cure from a hopelessly sick condition, Shashanka's sudden realisation of the importance of work and duty and Urmimala's maturing into the belief that separation is still tolerable, but not complications in one's own and near and dear one's lives.

It can be argued that along with *Shesher Kabita* (Farewell Song) and *Malancha* (Flower Garden), *Dui Bon* (Two Sisters) forms a trilogy where Tagore tried to depict the two dimensions of man's love for woman. In one manifestation she is the wife, in another the beloved. There are both similarities and dissimilarities between the women of these two moods. It is neither improper nor unjust on the part of a man to love both the wife and the beloved together, because there is no contradiction in these two kinds of love for woman. In the above-mentioned three novels, written almost back to back, Tagore presented this theory in different forms. In *Shesher Kabita* (Farewell Song) it was done in lyrical form; in *Dui Bon* (Two Sisters) through the realistic complications in man's life and easy solution from the woman's side; in *Malancha* (Flower Garden) through conflict in the woman's life and solution offered from the man's side.

In his biography of Rabindranath, Krishna Kripalani has briefly analysed the novel in these words, '*Two Sisters* is a short novel, mainly psychological in interest, dealing with the usual triangle, in this case two sisters in love with the same man. It is as if the author is trying to show that a man seeks in woman both mother and sweetheart... Human nature and society being what they are, a man cannot always have both and love is at best only a partial fulfillment. A heart that is alive cannot escape frustration. The situation in this novella is further complicated by the two rivals being sisters, both equally admirable, each in her own fashion. Tagore has tried to face boldly the psychological triangle caused by a conflict of loyalties, loyalty to married love, and loyalty to love, free and unfettered—without sentimentalising and without moralising.'

The structure and language of the novelette deserve a special mention. In the matter of construction what immediately attracts our attention is that Tagore here abandons the classical structure of the beginning, the middle and the end. Rather, he divides the book in four parts, a technique he first adopted in the *Chaturanga* (The Quartet). However, unlike in *Chaturanga*, the narration in *Dui Bon* is not from the angle of one observer. Here the omniscient author describes all the events under four chapters—Sharmila, Nirod, Urmimala and Shashanka. At the end of each chapter, the story-line changes course or a new formation is introduced. In the area of language also, Tagore totally forsakes the seriousness of expression and adopts an epigrammatic style. Whenever there arises a possibility of grave or sentimental situation, he drives it away by sharp epigrammatic comments or descriptions. The novel is thus totally steeped in the author's sunny chuckling irony and humour. This made the task of the present translator quite arduous. How far he has succeeded will be decided by the judgement of the discerning reader.

—Nirmal Kanti Bhattacharjee

TWO SISTERS

Women are of two types; that is what I've heard from some scholars.

One is of the mother category, the other is of a lover.

If a comparison with the seasons can be drawn, the mother is like the rainy season. She gives water, provides fruits, diffuses the heat, sends you cold showers from the high skies, removes dryness, fulfills your want.

And the beloved is like spring. Deep is her mystery, sweet is her charm, her fickleness creates ripples in your blood. The ripples reach that treasure-trove of your mind where a secret string in the golden *veena* silently waits for resonance, the resonance that vibrates in your entire body and mind with the message of the infinite.

Sharmila, the wife of Shashanka, is of the motherly type.

She has large, calm eyes; a deep, steady look; a body like moisture-laden new-formed clouds, plump and cool; a sunny vermilion mark on her forehead; the black border of her sari is broad; two solid *makar*-faced gold bracelets adorn her wrists. The language of her ornaments is not that of make-up, but of grace and sobriety.

There is not even a single nooky corner of her husband's life where the writ of her empire is not effective. The husband's mind has become careless due to this over-indulgence by the wife. It is the wife who discovers where the fountainpen has vanished in the cluttered table. It is the wife who finds out where Shashanka has misplaced the wrist-watch before going to the bathroom. When he is ready to go out wearing two socks belonging to two different pairs, it is the wife who notices and changes it. When he inadvertently mixes up the Bengali calendar with the Gregorian calendar and invites friends on a wrong date, it is the wife who manages to welcome and feed the unexpected guests. Shashanka knows in his heart that if a mistake happens in the affairs of daily life, his wife will rectify it in due time. Hence, committing mistakes has turned into his habit. The wife scolds him affectionately, 'I'm getting fed up with you. Won't you ever learn?' Had he really learnt, Sharmila's life would have turned into a barren land.

Suppose Shashanka is in a bridge party at a friend's place which goes on till midnight; suddenly the friends would laugh aloud saying, 'Here comes the court messenger with the summon. Your time is up, buddy.'

The well-known face of Mahesh, the faithful servant, appears. A pair of grey moustaches, a shock of dark hair, wearing a buniyan with a *gamchha* on his left shoulder, and a bamboo-stick in the arm-pit. Is the master here? The mistress is scared if any mishap happens during return so late at night. She has sent a lantern also.

A visibly annoyed Shashanka flings down his cards and gets up. The friends tease, 'Aha a lone unprotected man!' On return home, the tone in which Shashanka talks to his wife is neither soft nor low. Sharmila bears the rebuke silently. What can she do? She can't drive away the thought of imagined dangers that are lurking on the way to pounce on her husband.

Suppose, visitors are discussing serious business matters with Shashanka in their drawing room. Tiny slips would reach him from the inner-chamber of the house with regular frequency, 'Don't forget that you were unwell yesterday. It's time for your lunch.' Shashanka gets angry, but finally surrenders too. In utter dismay he once told his wife, 'Why don't you take shelter of a god like Mrs. Chakraborty. The quantum of your attention is too much for me to bear alone. It would be easier if I could share it with a god. A god would not object to any of your excesses, but a human is weak, you know!'

Sharmila responds, 'Oh, come on, don't you remember what happened to you when I once went to Haridwar with Kakababu?'

It is Shashanka himself who at that time told her with a lot of exaggeration how miserable his condition was. He knew that Sharmila would be as repentant as she would be happy at this exaggeration. He can't deny today what he himself once admitted with so much gusto.

Not only this, when the other day he sneezed a couple of times with the onset of a common cold, Sharmila made him swallow ten grains of quinine to arrest an imagined fever. This was followed by tea with basil-leaf juice. Shashanka could not protest. For, in a similar situation he once resisted the taking of quinine and later on had a high fever. This case history is written in Shashanka's medical records with indelible ink.

This affectionate eagerness of Sharmila for Shashanka's ease and comfort at home is matched by her alertness to preserve his prestige in the outside world. One remembers an instance.

Once they went for a holiday at Nainital. Railway compartment was reserved much in advance. At a junction, Sharmila had gone in search of food. Meanwhile two liveried army attendants were about to eject them from their compartment. The station master also came and declared that the compartment belonged to a famous General, it was given to Shashanka by mistake. With due reverence Shashanka immediately got up to look for another compartment elsewhere. When Sharmila boarded the train, she blocked the door and shouted spiritedly, 'Go, ask your General to come here. Let me see who can throw me out of my compartment.' Shashanka was still a government servant accustomed to play it safe by giving wide berth to the higher-ups. He tried to persuade Sharmila, saying, 'Aha, there are other compartments, why kick up a ruckus?' But Sharmila stood her ground. In the meantime, after finishing his lunch at the refreshment room, the General came out chewing a cheroot. Noticing the menacing stance of Sharmila from a distance, he decided to beat the retreat.

Shashanka asked his wife, 'Do you know how big the man is?'

Sharmila retorted, 'I don't care. At least, in my compartment he is not higher than you.'

Shashanka still persisted doubtfully, 'If he had insulted you?'

Sharmila's flat reply, 'What are you there for?'

Shashanka has an engineering degree from Shibpur Engineering College. He may be quite careless in the day-to-day household activities, but he is quite alert in his official work. For, the planetary constellation which ruthlessly governs his career is not his wife but the Saheb boss. When he was acting District Engineer, his impending promotion was thwarted by an upstart inexperienced young European officer. With strong recommendation from higher authorities, he came and usurped the rightful place of Shashanka and became his superior in the hierarchy.

Shashanka had realised that he was to run the show with this upstart seated above him like a dummy. The higher authority patted his back and said, 'Very sorry, Majumdar. I'll give you a higher placement as soon as possible.' Both of them belonged to the same freemason lodge.

Despite this consolation and assurance, the whole episode left a bad taste in Majumdar's mouth. He started acting peevish at home even at the slightest provocation. Suddenly, he discovered a patch of soot in a corner of his office room; suddenly he noticed a green cloth covering the table and realised that he hated the colour green. The bearer was sweeping the verandah and a dust-smoke was coiling up. Shashanka scolded him harshly. Inevitable dust flies during sweeping every day, but the scolding was new.

He did not share the news of his insult with his wife. He thought Sharmila might complicate the situation by confronting the authorities and picking up a quarrel. Especially, she was already angry with that Donaldson. Once, he punctured Shashanka's sola hat while firing a shot-gun at the monkeys in the garden of the Circuit House. Nothing serious happened, but could have happened. People said it was Shashanka who was at fault. This further aggravated her fury at Donaldson. The worst cause of her anger was that Shashanka's detractors enjoyed a derisive laughter by highlighting the uncharitable fact that the fire aimed at a monkey hit Shashanka.

Shashanka's wife herself found out the news of his supercession. She guessed from his recent behaviour that something somewhere had gone wrong. It did not take her long to unearth the reason. She did not take the path of constitutional agitation, but moved towards self-determination. She told her husband, 'Enough is enough. You should resign immediately.'

Such a course of action would definitely eject the leech of insult from his bosom. But in his eyes there was the security of the fixed salary and beyond that the golden hue of pension on the western horizon.

The year Shashankamouli climbed the summit of M.Sc degree, his marriage with Sharmila was solemnised. His father-in-law, Rajarambabu did not want to delay the auspicious occasion. It is with the wealthy father-in-law's support that Shashanka acquired his engineering degree. After that he progressed well in his career. His father-in-law was thus reassured about the financial solvency of his son-in-law. Sharmila also had nothing to complain about. She was in total charge of the material world of Shashanka's household. She had no children. By now they had virtually given up hope for a child. Her husband handed over his entire earning to her. When he himself needed money, he had to solicit it from his wife. In case of undue demand, Sharmila turned it down. He scratched his head and accepts the verdict. The disappointment was eminently compensated by some other sweet action of his wife.

Shashanka said, 'Giving up the job is no big deal for me. I'm concerned about you. You'll face discomfort.'

Sharmila replied, 'I'll have worse discomfort in swallowing the insult.'

Shashanka said, 'But I need a job. How can I run after uncertainty leaving something solid at hand?'

'The problem is, you don't consider any other alternative in this universe beyond a fixed job.'

'Good God! The universe is a huge concept. Who can survey its roads and maps? In which market do I find such a big binocular?'

'You don't need a big binocular. My cousin Mathurdada is a well-placed contractor at Calcutta. You can start a partnership business with him.'

'But the arrangement will be lopsided. My investment will be less. Weak partnership with a wife's brother results in loss of prestige.'

'Why should your investment be less? You know, father has left a sizeable sum in my name. The amount is increasing at compound interest in the bank. You don't have to be lower in the eye of your partner.'

'Impossible! That money is yours,' saying so Shashanka got up to leave. Some visitors were waiting outside.

Tugging at his clothes Sharmila made him sit again and said, 'I'm also yours.'

Then she commanded, 'Now, take out the fountainpen from your pocket. Here's the writing pad, write the resignation letter. I won't be at peace with myself before mailing it.'

'Me too,' saying so, Shashanka wrote out the resignation letter.

The very next day Sharmila left for Calcutta and put up at Mathurdada's house. She told him crossly, 'You never try to find out how your sister is doing.'

If it were a female at the receiving end, she would have retorted, 'Nor do you.' Such a response did not occur to a male. He admitted his lapse and said, 'I was really busy. There is absolutely no time for anything but work. Moreover, you people also keep moving from one place to another.'

Sharmila said, 'I read in the newspaper that you have got a huge contract of building a bridge somewhere in Mayurbhanj or Mathurganj. Felt so happy on reading it. Thought I should personally come and congratulate Mathurdada.'

'Not so fast, sister. There's still time to congratulate.'

From the discussion that followed it transpired that a lot of cash investment was necessary. It had been arranged that Mathur would work in partnership with a rich Marwarhi financier. But from the terms and conditions it was apparent that the lion's share of the profit would go to the Marwarhi financier. Mathur's share will be quite meagre. Hence he was trying to wriggle out of the agreement.

Sharmila got immensely concerned, 'Such a thing cannot be allowed to happen. It will be unfair if such a prestigious contract slips out of your hand. Whatever you say, I can't let this happen. We'll invest as your partner.'

Mathurdada's heart melted at Sharmila's generosity. After that it did not take long to draw up the agreement and fulfill other formalities.

The business went on in full swing. Earlier, in his job Shashanka had efficiently discharged his responsibilities. But that responsibility was limited. The owner was someone else. Now, he himself was the owner. Demand and due had converged. The weeks were no longer counted as a mix of work-days and holidays. Now time was a solid entity. Shashanka worked through day and night. He consoled himself: first I need to pay back my wife's debt. After that I can take it a little easy. Sola hat on the head, watch on the left wrist, Khaki trousers, rolled up shirt sleeves, tight waist-belt, sturdy pair of shoes, sunglass to protect the eyes—Shashanka took a real plunge in work. Wife's debt was at the point of being fully repaid, still there was no respite. His mind was charged up by then.

Earlier, the flow of income and expenditure was in one direction. Now, there were two, one towards the bank, other towards the household. As far as the second flow was concerned, Sharmila still ruled supreme. The mystery of credit and debit in that domain was beyond Shashanka's knowledge. But that leather-bound account book of business was like an inaccessible fort for Sharmila. That did not bother her. But as the orbit of her husband's business life fell outside her household pattern, her set rules and regulations started being frequently violated. She entreated, 'Please don't overstretch yourself, you will fall sick.' It fell on deaf ears. What is stranger, his health was not showing any sign of deterioration. Ignoring all her anxiety about his health, her concern for his lack of rest, her fuss over the minute details of his well-being and such other conjugal concerns, Shashanka would climb on his second-hand Ford car early in the morning and drive out to work. On return late in the afternoon, he would get a serious scolding from his wife, but would quickly finish his lunch and leave again.

One day, his car collided with another car. He himself escaped unhurt, but the car was severely damaged and sent to the workshop for repair. Sharmila said in a choked voice, 'From now onwards you won't drive yourself. Engage a driver.'

Shashanka laughed away the idea, 'Accident at the hand of somebody else is equally dangerous.'

One day while supervising over a repair work somewhere, a rusted nail of a packing box pierced through Shashanka's shoe and the sole of his foot. He went to the hospital, got first-aid and bandage over the wound and also an anti-tetanus injection. Sharmila cried in anguish and said, 'Lie down for a few days and take rest.'

Shashanka briefly said, 'I've works to do,' and left dragging his bandaged foot.

Sharmila did not dare insist any more. The male had found his forte. Beyond all arguments, all entreaties, there was only one decisive reply, 'I've tasks to do.'

Sharmila waits with unreasonable anxiety. If Shashanka is late to return, she thinks there must have been a car accident. If his face is flushed due to exposure to the sun, she thinks it must be influenza. Tentatively she hints at consulting a doctor, but stops short seeing her husband's expression. She does not even find enough courage in freely expressing her concern any more.

With the passage of time, Shashanka has become rough, rugged and sunburnt. Short tight dress, rare spare time, speedy movement, brief conversation in sparks. Sharmila's care for her husband tries to keep up with this fast pace. She keeps some food always warm near the stove, if the husband suddenly and untimely declares, 'I'm leaving. Will be late to return.' In the car she keeps some soda-water and some dry food in a tin-box. A bottle of eau de cologne is kept in a conspicuous spot in case he has a headache. When the car returns, she checks up to find that nothing was used. She feels sad. Washed and ironed clothes are kept neatly arranged every day in the bedroom, yet there is no time to change clothes at least four days a week. Consultations on different aspects of housekeeping have to be minimised, almost like urgent telegraphic exchanges, that too while Shashanka is on the move and Sharmila running behind him, 'O dear, listen to this, please.' The thin connection Sharmila had in their business was also disrupted as all her money had been repaid with interest. Shashanka has paid interest as per bank rate, taking proper receipt. Sharmila reproached, 'By God, the male species is incapable of totally submerging himself even in love. They reserve space, where their male vanity thrives.'

From his profit, Shashanka has built a house after his liking at Bhabanipur. Unique items of comfort and luxury are being regularly purchased. All for giving Sharmila a surprise. Sharmila also does not fail to be duly surprised. The engineer has set up a washing machine. Sharmila looks at it closely and praises it in superlative terms. But she muses inwardly. 'The clothes will go to the washerman tomorrow also, just as it goes today. I've understood the job of a washerman's donkey but can't understand that of science's donkey.' When she was shown the contraption for husking potato, she feigned amazement and said, 'Half the trouble of cooking potato will now be over.' It was later learnt that the instrument had found place among the junk along with broken kettle, punctured pot and such other discarded items.

When the construction of the house was finally complete, all Sharmila's pent-up affection moved over to this immoveable thing. It had an advantage: the body of brick and wood had infinite patience. In her relentless activity of designing and decorating, the two servants got exasperated. One finally left the job. Of course the centre of all this activity was Shashanka—his comfort. Barely did he sit in the drawing room these days; yet a number of cushions were arranged on the sofa to give respite to his fatigued backbone. Shashanka hardly entered the bedroom during the day, as in his new Sunday routine the day was nothing but the twin of Monday. He would spend the day in his office chamber poring over the plan of a building or pondering over the balance sheet of the business. Yet, a pair of pashmina chappals would be neatly arranged in front of the cushioned chair in the bedroom; a light silk kurta and a pleated dhoti would adorn the clothes hanger; fresh paan would be put in orderly fashion on the paan-stand. It needed some guts to intrude in the office chamber. Still, Sharmila entered it with a duster in Shashanka's absence and never gave up her attempt to bring a harmony between the objects to be discarded and those to be preserved.

Sharmila thus still serves Shashanka, but much of that service is offered behind the scene. The self-offering which she earlier made has now become indirect, almost symbolic, like decorating the house, tending the garden, visible perhaps in the silken cover of the chair on which Shashanka sits, in the flowering design of the pillow-cover on which Shashanka rests his head, in the jasmine stick placed in the blue crystal flower-vase.

She has had to place her offerings away from the altar with a lot of grief. The humiliation she had to suffer even a few days back had left a deep tear-stain in her eyes. That was nineteenth *Kartik*, Shashanka's birthday. The day of the greatest celebration in Sharmila's life. The house had been properly decked up. Friends had been invited as usual.

When Shashanka came home for lunch, he asked in surprise, 'What's up? Is it your doll's wedding today?'

'Cursed be my fate! Have you forgotten your birthday too? Come what may, you've to be at home this evening.'

'Business doesn't bow down to any other day but the day of death.'

'But I've already invited people. Please spare just one evening. I won't ask for anything again.'

'Look Sharmila, don't try to make me your toy in front of the whole world.'

Shashanka left in a huff. Sharmila shut the door of her bedroom and wept bitterly.

In the evening, her invitees came for the celebration. They all easily accepted the call of business. If it were the birthday of Kalidas, nobody would have accepted the excuse that he was busy writing the Third Act of *Shakuntala*. But business was business. There were a lot of jubilations. Nabubabu regaled everyone by imitating dialogues from theatre. Sharmila also joined in that laughter. Shashanka's birthday without Shashanka bowed fully prostrate before Shashanka's business.

Although Sharmila's sorrow knew no bounds, she still paid obeisance to the ensign of Shashanka's fast-moving chariot of work. She could not comprehend the nature of this work which did not care for anything, neither wife's entreaties, nor friends' invitations, nor one's own comfort. The male species paid respect to his own self by paying respect to his work. This was his self-offering to his own power. Standing on the threshold of her domestic chores, Sharmila respectfully watched the world of Shashanka's work. Its entity spread far and wide, beyond the borders of domesticity, to the distant shores of unknown oceans, dragging in so many strangers within its control. Man struggled every day with his destiny; if the tender arms of the woman created hurdles along this uneven journey, he promptly severed all ties with a rude jolt. Sharmila accepted this rudeness with reverence. At times she could not hold herself back; with a heart full of pathetic anxiety she tried to rectify a situation beyond her jurisdiction. Finally she had to give way with a painful heart. She returned hurt, but considered the hurt as her dessert. She implored her God, 'Protect Him.' This was one shelter where she had an easy passage.

NIROD

As the wealth of this family started accumulating in the bank and raced towards a six-digit figure, Sharmila was taken ill by a strange disease. She lost all her mobility. To understand the gravity of her illness, it is necessary to know the history of Sharmila's paternal family.

Her father Rajarambabu was a big zamindar with enormous landed property in Barishal at the estuary of the Ganga. Over and above, he had sizeable share in the ship-building business at Shalimar Ghat. He was born in the twilight hours of the last era and the beginning of this age. He had a formidable fame in wrestling, hunting and wielding the bamboo-stick. He was also an expert player of the *pakhwaj*. He could easily recite lines from the *Merchant of Venice*, *Julius Caesar* and *Hamlet*. Macaulay's English was his aspired ideal, Burke's oratory fascinated him. So far as Bengali literature was concerned, his respect ended with *Meghnadbadhkavya*. In his youth and middle age, he took alcohol and forbidden food as an indispensable part of entertainment, but had given it up all in old age. His dress was immaculate, his face handsome and serious, his physique tall and strong, and his mood courtly. He could not say 'no' to any solicitor. He did not have any devotion toward God or worship, but major pujas were celebrated with a lot of pomp and splendour at his home. The celebration would keep the ancestral glory intact, the real worship was for the women and others. He could have easily earned the title of Raja, but was indifferent to such trappings, as he believed that he should preserve with honour whatever title he had inherited from his father. He was a respected guest at the special chamber of the Government House. Highly placed British officers were regular patricipants in the champagne party accompanied with 'prasad' during the traditional Jagaddhatripuja at his place.

After Sharmila's marriage the widower Rajarambabu had his eldest son Hemanta and younger daughter Urmimala with him. The son was often described by his teachers as brilliant. His appearance was extremely attractive. There was no subject in which he would not get the highest mark. Moreover, he showed promise of being a chip off the old block in gymnastics as well. It goes without saying that a cluster of marriageable girls used to move in his orbit. But he was still indifferent to the idea of marriage. His present pre-occupation was towards earning a foreign degree. With this end in view, he started learning German and French.

With nothing better to do Hemanta simultaneously sought and found admission in law. This is when his intestine was afflicted with such a strange ailment which no doctor could diagnose. The secretive disease had as if taken shelter in his cast iron physique. It could neither be pin-pointed nor attacked. Rajaram had supreme confidence in a British doctor of the time who had formidable reputation in surgery. In his accustomed line of thinking he decided that the stomach had to be cut open and the affected organ removed by surgery. No trace of disease was found even after the deepest penetration of surgical instruments but the attempt proved fatal. Hemanta succumbed to the trauma. Rajarambabu was inconsolable in grief. It was not so much the death but the memory of cutting open such a beautiful strong body that clawed at his mind as if with the sharp nails of a violent black bird.

Nirod Mukherjee, a former classmate of Hemanta and now a medical intern was in attendance during his illness. He steadily maintained that the treatment was going in a wrong direction. He made his own diagnosis and advised a prolonged change to a dry climate. But Rajaram inherited the family tradition of unwavering faith on English physicians. He believed that only Englishmen could be a proper match in the fight with Lord Yama, the God of Death. Now, his respect and affection for Nirod increased beyond all measure. His younger daughter Urmi also suddenly felt that this man had uncommon talent. She told her father, 'Look father, what self-confidence! How fearlessly he expressed his doubt in the face of such a famous British doctor!'

The father said, 'Medical science is not just a discipline. Some people have rare divine instinct for it. It seems Nirod possesses this instinct.'

Their respect began with an incident, at the reaction of grief, at the pain of repentance. And then without waiting for any other proof, it kept on magnifying on its own.

One day Rajaram told his daughter, 'Look Urmi, I always seem to hear Hemanta calling and urging me, 'Mitigate man's suffering from disease'. I have decided to build a hospital in his name.'

In her natural enthusiasm Urmi responded, 'That would be great, father! Please send me to Europe so that I can come back as a doctor and take charge of the hospital.'

The words touched Rajaram's heart. He said, 'Yes, the hospital would be a public trust, you will be its chief trustee. Hemanta has suffered a lot. He loved you very dearly. This auspicious work would give him peace in the other world. It is you who nursed him in his death bed; that service will now extend further in scope.'

The old man did not even think for once that the girls from such respectable families were not sent abroad to study medicine. He felt in his heart what it meant to save somebody from the clutches of a disease. His son did not survive, but as if there would be a compensation if other people's sons survive, as if the grief then would be somewhat lessened. He told his daughter, 'First complete the science education in the university here, then Europe calls you.'

Henceforth, a thought kept recurring in Rajaram's mind. It was about that young man, Nirod. He was a gem of a boy. The more Rajaram saw him the more impressed he was. Although he had already passed the medical examination, Nirod was relentlessly swimming in the ocean of medical science all day and night. He was young, but no entertainment tempted him. He kept track of whatever new experiments happened on the subject, studying them and thus neglecting his medical practice. He had only contempt for those who had done well in practice. He would say, the fools prosper, the deserving wins accolades. He must have stolen the sentence from some book.

At last, one day Rajaram told Urmi, 'I've given it a thought. I feel it would be best if you work as Nirod's companion in our hospital. This arrangement will make my mind free of all concern. After all, Nirod is the most eligible bachelor around.'

Rajaram had great respect for Hemanta's opinion. He used to say, imposing a match on the daughter ignoring her choice was barbarism. Rajaram once argued that marriage in our society was not an individual matter, there were two families involved in it. Hence it became at times necessary to be guided by experience rather than by one's own will. Whatever argument he might have made, whatever might have been his own opinion, his affection and respect for Hemanta was so deep that finally Hemanta's will had the way.

Nirod Mukherjee was a frequent visitor to this house. Hemanta nicknamed him owl. He would explain—this fellow is of the mythological type, ageless, full of wisdom: hence, I call him owl, the carrier of Goddess Minerva.

Nirod would often have tea with Hemanta and the two had tumultuous debates over various issues. He must have noticed Urmi, but had not shown any inclination to get acquainted with her. For, he could only discuss serious things, but did not know how to make small talk. Even if the heat of youth was present in him, the light was missing. He felt smug in showing disdain for those young men who had a natural expression of youthful disposition. For all these reasons, no one dared to include him among the group of Urmi's suitors. And yet this seeming indifference coupled with the cause of the hospital created an adoration in Urmi's mind.

When Rajaram made it clear that he would be happy if Urmi agreed to marry Nirod, she nodded her head in acquiescence. Her only condition was that the marriage would be solemnised only after her education both here and abroad were over. The father said, 'Fair enough. I would only be relieved if the match is declared final on mutual consent.'

Nirod was quick to agree, but his apparent demeanour made it seem as though marriage was a great sacrifice on the part of a scientist, almost akin to suicide. Perhaps as a mitigating factor, he imposed the condition that from then onwards he would govern Urmi's studies and all other matters. In other words, he would himself mould Urmi as his future wife. Even that process would follow a scientific discipline, which was the first principle in his laboratory.

Nirod told Urmi, 'Birds and beasts have come out of Nature's workshop. Finished product. But man is just raw material. It has been left onto man himself to give it a shape.'

Urmi softly replied, 'That's fine. Go ahead with your experiment. There's no objection from my side.'

Nirod said, 'You have various kinds of energy. These have to be channelised towards one goal of your life. Only then your life will acquire some meaning. All the dissipated energy needs to be condensed to a dynamic essence, the resultant unit can be called moral organism, you know.'

Urmi was duly impressed. Many young men in the past had joined them for tea or in the tennis court, but none had ever uttered anything thoughtful. If anyone else had, they would yawn. As a matter f fact, Nirod had a way of stating deep thoughts tellingly. Whatever he said, Urmi would find it intellectually stimulating.

Rajaram invited his elder son-in-law too. He wanted them to know each other well through occasional lunches and dinners at his place. Shashanka told Sharmila, 'The fellow is insufferably precocious. He considers all of us his students, that too of the last bench.'

Sharmila laughed and commented, 'This is your jealousy. I find him all right.'

Shashanka merrily retorted, 'Really! How about swapping roles with your sister?'

Sharmila rose to the occasion, 'Well, I'm sure, in that case you will feel eminently relieved.'

Not that Nirod also had developed any great fellow-feeling towards Shashanka. He thought, 'He is just a mechanic, not a scientist. He has efficient hands, but where's the head?'

Shashanka often teased his sister-in-law about Nirod, 'It's time to change your old name.'

'In English fasion?'

'No, in pure Sanskrit fasion?'

'Like?'

'Say, Bidyutlata, streak of lightning. Nirod will love it. He has encountered this in his laboratory, now he can confine it at home.'

He mused inwardly, 'Yes, it is a name that suits this girl.' At the same time, he felt a little sad, 'Alas! Such a girl will belong to such a great pig!' It is difficult to venture a guess belonging to whom would have satisfied Shashanka and consoled him.

Rajaram breathed his last after some time. Nirodnath, the would-be-husband of Urmi took full charge of his affairs.

Urmimala looked more beautiful than she actually was. She radiated with restless freshness both in body and mind. She had a healthy curiosity about everything. Although she studied science, she had no less interest in literature. She was always ready to go to the field to watch a football match; she never considered watching a movie any lower form of entertainment. If a physics scholar from a foreign university would give a lecture in Presidency College, she would be invariably present there. She would intently listen to the light songs in radio; maybe she would say, 'Inane! Inane!' but there was no dearth of curiosity either. If a bridegroom was proceeding for marriage, his long entourage revelling with dances and drumbeats, she would rush to the veranda to see it. She loved to visit the zoological garden time and again and especially enjoyed standing in front of the cage of the monkeys. When her father used to go to the pond for angling the fish she would go and sit near him. She played tennis quite well and was a champion badminton player.

All this she had learnt with her brother. She was not a good singer, but was a reasonably good sitar player. As a member of the audience you won't be sure if that music looked better or sounded better. Her dress sense was immaculate. She knew how to look appealing without looking ostentatious. She was never in short of conversation, never needed any reason to laugh out heartily. She was wonderful company and had mastered the art of plugging all the gaps in a gathering. Only in the presence of Nirod she changed into a different person as if the sail of the boat had suddenly lost wind and made it float at a slow pace.

It was generally believed that Urmi's nature was like her brother, full of life and vitality. Urmi knew that her brother had liberated her mind. Hemanta used to say, 'Our houses are like moulds, they make us like clay models. This is why the foreign pipers have played thirty-three crore puppets so easily for so long. When my time comes, I will go out like Kalapahad and destroy all the social idolatry.' His time never came, but he had left Urmi's mind very fresh and green.

The trouble started with the method of work. Nirod's method was extremely disciplined. He prepared a chart for Urmi's study. He gave her a proper sermon, 'Look Urmi, don't let your mind spill again and again on your way. For, in that case at the end of the journey, you may find the pot empty.'

He would analyse her nature critically like this—'You float around restlessly like a butterfly, hence can't collect anything. One has to be like a bee. They account for every moment. After all, life is not a train of luxury!'

Nirod had recently got some books on educational philosophy from the Imperial Library which contained such ideas. His language was the language of books, for he did not have his own language. However, Urmi had no doubt that it is she who was guilty. She had a noble objective. Yet, her mind was easily diverted to this way or that. Whereas she had the burning example of Nirod before her eyes—what determination, what unwavering aim, what stiff resistance to all kinds of entertainment! If he found any novel or light reading book on Urmi's table, he would immediately confiscate it. One evening, he came to Urmi's house only to find that she had gone to watch the evening show of Sullivan's *Mikado Opera* at the English theatre. She never missed such chances when her brother was alive. That day, Nirod scolded her severely. In a grave tone he hit her where it hurt most, 'Look, you've taken a vow to fulfill the promises of your brother's life with all your might. Have you already begun to forget it?'

Urmi felt extremely repentant. She thought, 'What uncommon insight this man has! It's true that the intensity of my grief has considerably lessened. Even I myself couldn't realise it! Curse me, I'm so fickle-minded!' She started being alert and careful; banished all colour and make-up from her appearance; started wearing ordinary off-white saris; gave up her urge for consuming chocolates, though a number of them were piled in the cupboard; confined her rebellious mind to the dry dreary discourse of duty only. Sharmila was alarmed. She tried to reason with her sister. Shashanka used the choicest English epithets towards Nirod which were not at all palatable to the ear.

Shashanka and Nirod were alike in one point. When Shashanka felt a strong urge to hurl abuses, he switched over to

English. When Nirod felt an urge to give high-falutin sermons, he also switched over to English. Nirod strongly disapproved of Urmi's visits to her sister's place on festivals and invitations. Not only did she visit, she was very eager to visit. Somehow Nirod found her pleasant relationship with Shashanka's family a threat to his relationship with her.

One day, Nirod seriously addressed Urmi on this count. He said, 'Look Urmi, please don't mind my saying what I'm going to say. I've no other alternative. Given my sense of responsibility towards you, it is my duty to pronounce even the unpalatable truth. I warn you, your rubbing shoulders with Shashankabu and his family is detrimental to your character building. You are blinded by the infatuation of familial relations, but I can clearly visualise a catastrophe coming out of this relationship.'

Whatever was meant by Urmi's character, the agreement paper of its first mortgage was in the safe-vault of Nirod. It is Nirod who would suffer loss by any damage in that character. As a result, Urmi's visits to Bhabanipur became few and far between. She refused invitations on some excuse or other. Urmi considered this self-denial as a repayment of debt. After all, Nirod had agreed to compromise his scientific quest to some extent by accepting the responsibility of her life.

Urmi was gradually coming to terms with her suffering at forgoing many tempting attractions of life. Still, a melancholy overtook her from time to time which she could not just dismiss as her fickleness of mind. Nirod only governed her, but never for a moment adored her. Her heart intensely longed for this adoration. In absence of it the sweetness of her mind could not express itself to the full. All her duties turned dry, lifeless. There were moments when she imagined Nirod's eyes betraying a softness, as if the deepest mystery of life was about to be revealed. But God knew, even if the depth of that pathos lurked somewhere in the mind, Nirod did not know its language. And since he did not know it, he rubbished the very desire to express it. He considered it the demonstration of his inner strength that he went back without giving tongue to his stirred soul. He would say, 'I'm not given to sentimentality.' Urmi felt like crying, but she had brought herself to such a state that she reverentially bowed even before this conduct and accepted it as heroism. Then she started punishing her weak mind in a severe manner. But despite all her attempts of uprightness, at times it became evident to her that she had desperately held on to somebody else's resolve, because her own resolve of a hard task that she accepted in the wake of a devastating grief had already become weak.

Nirod clearly told her, 'Look Urmi, you better get it clear that you won't ever receive from me the kind of adulation that ordinary girls receive from the male-suitors. What I will bring to you is much more valuable than all these make-believe words.'

Urmi sat silently, her head bowed. She grudgingly thought, 'Can there be no secret from this man?'

She found it almost impossible to suppress her real self. She went up to the roof and loafed around alone. The evening dust settled down. The sun moved across the high and low buildings of the city and set beyond the masts of the ships anchored at the distant ghat of the Ganga. Multi-coloured strips of cloud fenced the sky at the border of the day. Gradually the fence melted away and the moon came up above the dome of the church. In her subdued light the city looked like a dream, like a ghost-city.

An uneasy question took shape in her mind—is life really so stiff, so hard? Is it so niggardly that it won't allow any respite, any fun? Suddenly her mind rebels, she feels like shouting out in mischief, 'I don't care. I won't abide by anything.'

URMIMALA

The research project which Nirod had been conducting was now over. He sent the thesis to a science society in Europe. They appreciated it and offered him a scholarship. He decided to go abroad and obtain a degree from a foreign university.

There was no sad dialogue at the time of farewell. He just repeatedly hammered on, 'I'm leaving. What I'm afraid of is that your grip on the task at hand may loosen.'

Urmi replied, 'Don't worry on that count.'

Nirod declared, 'I will leave a detailed note on how you should bear yourself out and how you should conduct your studies.'

Urmi assured him, 'I will follow this in toto.'

'I plan to shift those worthless books from your almirah to my house and keep them under lock and key.'

'Take them away.' Urmimala handed over the key to him. Nirod gave the sitar a stern look also, but stopped short of saying anything.

At last, due to sheer sense of responsibility he had also to say, 'I'm afraid if you again start visiting Shashankababu's place regularly, then your determination is bound to weaken. Please don't misunderstand me. I've nothing against Shashankababu. He is basically a very good person. I've seen very few Bengalis with so much drive and acumen for business. His only fault is that he doesn't believe in any ideal. Believe me, sometimes I feel scared for him.'

In course of this conversation, many other faults of Shashanka came to light and Nirod could not suppress his anxiety for what would happen when the faults which were latent would now manifest themselves with advancing age. At the same breath, he would also like to admit without reservation that Shashanka was a good man. But at the same time, he would want to alert Urmi that she should protect herself against his company and against the philistine atmosphere of his house. It would be a disaster if Urmi's mind came down to their level.

Urmi asked, 'Why are you getting so worked up?'

'Would you like to hear the real reason? Promise me that you won't mind.'

'It's from you that I've got the strength to hear truth. I know it's not easy, still I can bear it.'

'Then listen. I've noticed that there's a similarity of nature between you and Shashankababu. His mind is very shallow. That's what appeals to you, isn't it?'

Urmi thought, 'Is the man omniscient?' No doubt, she tremendously liked her brother-in-law. The main reason for her liking was that Shashanka knew how to laught out loudly and heartily, knew how to make mischief, to tease and provoke. And also knew for certain which flower Urmi liked and which colour of sari she preferred.

Urmi replied truthfully, 'Yes, it's true that I like him.'

Nirod said, 'The love of Sharmiladidi is soft and deep, her service is almost like propitiation. She never takes leave from her duties. It's because of her influence that Shashankababu has learnt to work with attention and commitment. But the day you go to Bhabanipur, his mask falls off. He starts shadow-boxing with you, he eases out your hair clips, untangles and smoothens your hair down, snatches your book and puts it on the almirah above your reach. Despite work at hand, he suddenly feels an urge to play a hand in tennis.'

Urmi had to concede that she liked Shashankada all the more because he created such a ruckus around her. Her own childlike urges came to the fore when she was with him. And she herself inflicted no less trouble on him. Sharmila smiled an indulgent smile when she observed this mutual teasing of each other. At times, she even pulled them up mildly.

Nirod concluded the argument saying, 'You should be with such people where your own childish nature does not get boosting. If I were around, this wouldn't have been a problem. For, my nature is diametrically opposite of yours. I could never bring myself up to spoiling you mind just to entertain you.'

With head bowed Urmi said, 'I'll remember your words.'

Nirod said, 'I'm leaving a few books for you. Carefully go through the chapters that I've especially marked for you. These would stand you in good stead in future.'

Urmi needed this help. Of late, she had often been suffering from self-doubt. She would think, 'Perhaps it was a mistake I committed in the rush of excitement. Perhaps studying medicine is against my grain.'

After Nirod's departure, Urmi made her life totally regimented. She would go to college, but at other times she would almost confine herself to a Zenana. After a day's toil in the college when her mind craved for some diversion, she would force herself to sit at the study table again. Study would not progress, her distracted mind would move around the same page over and over again. Yet, she refused to give up. Because of his absence, Nirod's will-force started imposing itself all the more on her mind.

She hated herself most when during work, happy memories of her earlier fun-filled life would come back again and again. She had a lot of admirers among young men. She had ignored some, but felt drawn towards a few too. It did not evolve into love, but the desire for love itself was like some vernal breeze blowing across her mind. She would hum a romantic tune to herself absent-mindedly, copy a romantic poem in her note-book. When she felt too distracted, she would sit down to play the sitar. On some evenings, when she was trying to concentrate on a book, she would be startled to realise that her mind was wandering to someone from the distant past who adored her but whose excessive attention in those days used to annoy her. Perhaps the pathos of that unrequited attention today touched a chord in her discontented mind, just as the momentary light touch of a butterfly's wings intimates the flower of the advent of spring.

The more she tried to forcefully banish these thoughts from her mind, the more they would come back to her on a rebound. She had kept a photograph of Nirod on her desk-top. She gazed at it from time to time. If reflected the brilliance of intellect, but not the eagerness of a lover. He did not call her, then whom would she respond to? She fortified her heart by repeating time and again, 'What talent! What dedication! What pure character! How fortunate I am!'

It has to be said that Nirod had been victorious at least on one front. When he was engaged to Urmi, Shashanka and a few others of his ilk laughed in derision. They said, Rajarambabu was a simple man. He had easily mistaken Nirod to be an idealist. But all his bombasts would not hide the fact that his idealism was secretly laying eggs within Urmi's bank balance. Of course, he was making a sacrifice, but the temple of the god to whom the sacrifice was being made lay in the Imperial Bank. We tell our fathers-in-law that we need money and that money will not go down the drain. It will ultimately augur well for their daughters. But this man pretended nobility and declared that he would marry only for a noble cause. Later on, the aims and objectives of the cause would be translated in the father-in-law's cheque books.

Nirod anticipated such talks. He told Urmi, 'I've a pre-condition to marriage. I'll not accept a single penny from your side. I'll solely go by my own earning.'

The father-in-law offered to send him to Europe. He flatly refused. As a result, he had to wait long for an opportunity to study abroad. He told Rajarambabu, 'Please donate in your daughter's name whatever money you want to donate for building up the hospital. When I take charge of that hospital, I'll not take any remuneration for that. I'm a physician. Earning my livelihood is not a problem for me.'

Looking at this supreme detachment, Rajarambabu's respect for Nirod further increased and Urmi felt terribly proud. This ostentatious demonstration of so-called detachment suddenly made Sharmila averse and allergic to Nirod. She commented, 'Let me see how long he can maintain this vanity.' Since then whenever Nirod would start mouthing his high-sounding rhetoric, Sharmila would simply get up and storm out of the place. The sound of her footsteps echoed angrily for some distance. She did not openly say anything just for the sake of Urmi, but her disdain was not a carefully kept secret either.

At the beginning, Nirod used to send four-five page letters to Urmi from abroad. These were full of advice and guidelines. Then suddenly he surprised her by sending a telegram. He needed a large sum of money for pursuing further studies. The pride which was Urmi's mainstay so long was somewhat hurt, but she also felt some consolation in her mind. The more days passed and the longer Nirod's absence grew, the more Urmi's suppressed nature sought an outlet from the rigours of discipline. She indulged in occasional escapades, then suffered from remorse. Hence, in such moments of self-deprecation, providing financial support to Nirod brought her some mental satisfaction.

Urmi handed over the telegram to their estate manager and said, 'Kaka, the money....'

He remarked, 'I'm puzzled. We thought your money is untouchable for him.'

The manager was not particularly fond of Nirod.

Urmi protested, 'But in a foreign country....' She did not complete the sentence.

The manager-uncle quipped, 'I know that the character of this country may change in a foreign country, but how are we going to keep pace with that change, dear?'

Urmi weakly said, 'He may face trouble if he doesn't get the money.'

'Ok, dear, I'll send the money. Don't worry. But let me also warn you that this is the beginning, not the end.'

That it was not the end was proved by the need for a larger amount. This time it was for the treatment of some health problem. The manager gravely said, 'Perhaps you should consult Shashankababu.'

Urmi's reaction was immediate, 'Whatever you do, please keep this information away from Didi.'

'I am not enjoying taking this responsibility alone.'

'In any case, this money will be his, today or tomorrow.'

'But we must ensure that the money is not wasted.'

'Shouldn't we think about his health?'

'Ill health has many categories. One wonders which category this one belongs to. If he returns here, change of weather might help. Shall I send him the passage money?'

The proposal of return made Urmi extremely restless. She was afraid lest Nirod's lofty aim was thwarted because of her.

Kaka said, 'I'm sending money this time, but I guess this will further deteriorate the health of Daktarbabu.'

Radhagobinda was a close relative of Urmi. Noting the slant in Kaka's comment, he thought 'I must confide in Didi'. On the other hand, he was repeatedly pushing his own guilt-conscience, asking, 'Why am I not sufficiently aggrieved?'

About this time, Sharmila's illness was turning to be a cause of worry. Especially scary was the memory of the fate of her brother. Many specialist doctors were trying to get at the root of the disease. Sharmila smiled wearily, saying, 'The criminal will escape from the hands of the CID, only the innocent will suffer.'

A concerned Shashanka said to doctors, 'Let the investigation continue as per usual procedure, but I do not want any undue stress caused to the patient.'

At that time, Shashanka got two major contracts. One was at a jutemill on the banks of the Ganga. The other near Tollygunj, at the new outhouse of the zamindar of Mirpur. The work of the jutemill's labour colony was to be completed within three months. A few tubewells were also to be bored at different places. He had no time to spare. Yet, he was often detained due to Sharmila's ailment. This was putting additional stress on his mind.

During their long married life, Shashanka never had to worry about Sharmila's health. She was hardly ever taken ill. Hence, Shashanka was anxious and fidgety like a child at this illness of Sharmila. He would bunk work and sit near her bed helplessly. Touching her head lightly, he would ask, 'How are you today?'

Sharmila replied immediately, 'I'm fine. Please don't worry unnecessarily about me.'

Shashanka badly needed to believe in her reply and said, 'I have got a big deal from the king of Dhenkanol. I will have to go and discuss the plan with the Dewan. Will come back as soon as I can, and most certainly before the doctor visits.'

Sharmila said reassuringly, 'Please do not spoil your work in haste. I understand that you need to go to their state. Here I have a number of attendants. I shall be all right.'

Shashanka's mind was day and night engaged in the mighty ambition of building up huge wealth. His attraction was not wealth *per se*, but the greatness associated with it. It should be the objective of a man to build up something big. You can neglect money or wealth as long as it is a means to just livelihood. But when its pinnacle is made high and mighty, people start respecting it. Not because they benefit from it but just the sight of the spectacle fills the heart. When Shashanka was anxiously sitting at the bedside of Sharmila, he was also simultaneously worrying about this unexpected hurdle at his work. Sharmila was aware that Shashanka's anxiety about work was not a slight for her, it was for the celebration of manliness which fulfills itself in achieving high, beginning from scratch. She was proud of this success of Shashanka. Hence, she did not like the fact that her husband would be slack in work for attending to her sick-bed, though it made her inwardly happy. So, she used to repeatedly send him away to work.

On the other hand, Sharmila was distraught at the fact that she was unable to discharge her household duties properly. She was bed-ridden, who knew what the maids and servants and cooks were doing? She was sure, bad quality ghee was being used in cooking, hot water was not being supplied to the bathrooms in time, the bed sheets were not being changed in due time, the drains were not being regularly cleared by the sweepers. And then, she was well aware of the problems that ensued if the clothes from the washerman were not properly checked against the list. Feeling restless, she would force herself to get up and go to supervise. The pains relapsed, the temperature rose. The doctor was at a loss thinking what went wrong.

At last, Sharmila sent for her younger sister Urmimala. She said, 'Take leave from your college for some time, dear and save my household. Otherwise, I would not even die in peace.'

Those of you who are reading this story must be smiling knowingly at this point about the shape of things to come. One does not require to be very intelligent to guess it. What is to happen, happens, and that is good enough. Also, there is no reason to think that fate will play the game with the cards close to the chest and keeping Sharmila totally in the dark.

Urmi felt very enthusiastic at the thought of going to nurse her elder sister. She had to relegate all other work behind for the call of this duty. Moreover, she told herself that this work of nursing would stand her in good stead when she pursued her future medical profession.

With great aplomb, she collected a leather-bound note book in which charts and diagrams were there to record the daily rise and fall of temperature and other symptoms. Lest the doctor dismiss her as ignorant, she decided she would study everything about Sharmila's ailment. The subject of her M.Sc course was Physiology, hence it would not be much difficult to understand the terminologies of the disease. In short, having convinced herself that nursing her sister would in no way derail her from her studies, rather it would enhance her prospects further, she arrived at Bhabanipur with a bag full of books and papers. But she did not get much scope to study any thick medical book about her sister's disease, for the specialist doctors also could not diagnose Sharmila's real illness.

Urmi thought that she had got the right to rule. So, she gravely told Sharmila, 'Didi my duty is to see that you abide by all the instructions of the doctors. So, you will have to listen to my every word, mind you.'

Didi was amused by her over-serious demeanour. She smiled and said, 'Which Guru taught you to be so serious? You seem over-enthusiastic because of the new initiation. Come on, I have summoned you so that you will listen to my word. Your hospital is not yet built. My household is readymade. For the time being, take responsibility of that. Let your Didi enjoy a break.'

Sharmila almost forced Urmi away from her sick-bed.

Now, she was Didi's representative in her home-kingdom. Anarchy was rampant there, it needed to be rectified immediately. One man was seated at the summit of this household. There should not be any lapse in serving him. This should be the only objective for all other inhabitants of this kingdom, small or big. Sharmila could never forget that the man was totally helpless and ridiculously clueless about the domestic chores. She felt like laughing and yet her mind became full of indulgent compassion when she would notice that his shirt-sleeve caught fire from the burning cheroot and he was totally unware of it. The engineer would wash his face in the corner basin of the bedroom in the morning and rush for work leaving the tap open. On return, he would find the room deep in water, the expensive carpet totally damaged. In fact, Sharmila had objected when this tap was being installed there. She knew that the hands of this man would cause some calamity or the other with water in the bedroom. But the celebrated engineer had a way of convincing others by talking about the advantage of scientific facilities and thereby complicating matters. Once, just by whim he built a stove totally with his own original plan. It had one opening this side, another that side; one chimney this side, another that side.

On one side, the fire would rise without any waste of energy; on another downslide ashes would be simultaneously eliminated. Over and above, there were numerous holes and cabins and cavities for heating, warming, boiling, frying etc. From the language of the demonstration of the machine, it was obvious that it was not exactly meant for use but for maintaining peace and solidarity. This is how the adults play. If you resist, there will be huge tantrums. And yet, they forget the whole thing after a few days. They are not happy with the conventional method, and would want to create something strange. It is the duty of the wife not to humour them in their caprice, but to manage her own business according to her own judgment. So long, Sharmila had happily carried out this business of tending the husband.

Such a long journey. Sharmila could not even imagine Shashanka's world without herself in it. Now she was afraid if the messanger of Death would come and separate the world with its holder. She even feared that even after her death, her abodeless soul would fret at any physical discomfort of Shashanka. Urmi was a godsend. She was not as calm and composed like her. But still she was managing all the works on her behalf. In any case, all these works belonged to the woman's domain. Without that soft feminine touch, the day-to-day life of men became bereft of all beauty and essence. So, when Urmi peeled an apple with a knife in her beautiful hands, when she arranged the kernels of an orange on one side of a white stone dish, when she carefully placed the seeds of a ripe pomegranate on it, Sharmila as if realised herself through her sister. Lying on bed, she would constantly direct Urmi to do this or that.

'Urmi, fill up his cigarette case.'

'Don't you see that his handkerchief has become dirty. Change it.'

'Look here, the pair of shoes are covered with cement and dirt. Can't you remember to ask the bearer to clean it?'

'Time to change the pillow-covers, dear.'

'Throw away those torn papers in the waistbin.'

'Urmi, please go to his office room once. I am sure he had left the key to the cash-box on the desk.'

'Don't forget it's time to plant the cauliflower plants.'

'Ask the gardener to prune the branches of the rose-plants.'

'Look, there is lime-stain on the back of the coat. Wait for a moment–what's the hurry–Urmi, please brush the stain out of the coat.'

Urmi was basically the studious type, not the one accustomed to domestic chores. Yet, she was enjoying all this. Her life was governed by a strong regimen; she tasted liberty stepping out of it. The thread of anxiety and penance that ran through this household did not touch her. That thread was running through her didi's mind. For her, these chores were a game, a kind of holiday, purposeless arrangements. It was a totally different world from where she had been so far. Here, no index finger pointed towards a goal in front of her. Yet, the days were full of tasks; those tasks were also of varied nature. She committed mistakes; these were lapses, but she did not have to seriously answer for them. Even if Didi tried to pull her up a bit, Shashanka would laugh it away, as if there is a special humour in Urmi's lapses. As a matter of fact, the gravity of responsibility was missing from their household now. The situation was slack to the extent that the slips and mistakes did not seem to matter anymore. It was this which was of great comfort and amusement to Shashanka. As if a permanent picnic was going on. That Urmi was not perturbed nor sorry nor ashamed by anything, that she laughed with abandon at everthing made light of Shashanka's burden of work. He was eager to return home immediately after his work was over, at times even before it was over.

It has to be conceded that Urmi was not an expert housekeeper, but it was obvious that she had filled up a huge gap in this house, if not by her work at least by virtue of her own being. It is difficult to pin-point the exact nature of that gap. For example, when Shashanka returned home he felt a surge of holiday spirit in the ambience. That spirit did not lie only in the attentive service, nor just in the pleasure of leisure, it had its own manifest essence. In fact, the joy of Urmi's own vacation had fulfilled all the vacuum here and made the day and night full of mirth and gaiety. This incessant joyousness created waves in the blood of work-weary Shashanka. On the other hand, the direct feeling that Shashanka was happy with Urmi made Urmi also happy in turn. Urmi had never experienced this happiness in her life so far. The fact that she could make someone delighted just by dint of her existence was so long suppressed. And it was this which had reduced her real glory.

Now, the lady of the house considered it a rather minor matter whether Shashanka's food and drink were being served as per his regular routine or if he was receiving the supply of the right comfort-items at the right time. What was more important was that he was in a happy and expansive mood without any particular reason. She would then tell Sharmila, 'Why do you get so worked up with the nitty-gritty? It is not bad if there is occasional deviation from habit; one feels happy at that.'

Shashanka's mind was now like a river in between ebb and tide. The dynamics at work looked quite stable. One did no longer hear about such anxiety that a little delay or a slight obstacle would create any heavy loss. If Shashanka expressed anything like that, Urmi would immediately make light of it. She would laugh at his serious face and say, 'Did your *juju* come today, that alien middle-man with green *pagdi*? Has he threatened you?'

A surprised Shashanka would ask, 'How do you know about him?'

'I know him quite well. When you were not at home the other day, he was sitting by the verandah. It was I who chatted him up and kept him engaged. His home is in Bikaner. His wife died of an accident when their mosquito-net caught fire. He is now looking for another suitable match.'

'Good God, he would now calculate time and visit only when I am not home. As long as he does not find another bride, he will keep dreaming with you.'

'Let me know what work is to be extracted from him. The way he warms up to me, I feel I will be able to manage it.'

These days, Shashanka did not seem to be unduly distracted if the balance sheet of profit and loss looked a little slow in growth. It was also hitherto not known that he was so keen on tuning in the radio in the evening. These days, Shashanka did not think it a trifle matter or a waste of time if Urmi called him out for nothing. One early morning he had to go to Dumdum airport to see how the aeroplanes took flight. Scientific curiosity was not the only reason for that. He even made a shopping trip to New Market for the first time in his life. Earlier, Sharmila used to go there at times to buy vegetables, fruits, fish and meat. She knew that it was specifically her department and had never thought of asking Shashanka to accompany her on these trips. But Urmi did not go there to shop; she would walk around, touch and feel a few samples, and bargain about the price of a few others. If Shashanka tried to purchase any item she gave particular attention to, she would snatch his purse and keep it in her vanity bag.

Urmi did not care for the importance of Shashanka's work. Once or twice she got serious scolding for distracting him unnecessarily. The result was so catastrophic that Shashanka had to give her double time to appease her.

On one side Urmi's tears, on the other indispensable work-pressure. To avoid crisis, Shashanka tried to finish all work in his office-chamber itself, before returning home. But it became impossible to stay there as the evening progressed. If for some reason he was late to return home, Urmi would stop talking to him. Her moist eyes and her *abhimaan* pleased Shashanka inwardly in a mysterious way. With an innocent face, he would say, 'Urmi if you don't want to talk, I will co-operate with your non-cooperation. But, by God, at least we can play together, can't we?' Then he would come out with his tennis racket. In the match, Shashanka deliberately let her win. Next morning, looking at the pending work, he would repent for the wasted time.

On one holiday afternoon, as Shashanka was busy poring over a particularly complicated diagram with red and blue pencils in the right hand and ruffling his hair with his left, Urmi came and said, 'I have fixed with that agent of yours that he would take me out to the Pareshnath temple today. Please come with me.'

Shashanka pleaded with her, 'Sorry, dear! I can't leave now.'

Urmi was never impressed by the importance of work. She said, 'You have no qualm in leaving an unprotected girl at the hand of the green-*pagdiwala* man! Where is your chivalry gone?'

At last, Shashanka had to abandon work and drive her out to Pareshnath. Sharmila would be very irritated if she heard of any such disturbance in Shashanka's life. For, she believed that women should never make any untoward entry into the domain of men's work, which was their 'sadhana'. She had always considered Urmi childish, and even indulged her. But the office and the household were not playing fields. So, she would summon Urmi and rebuke her quite sternly. Such rebuffs could have worked, but Shashanka, having heard his wife's angry loud voice, would himself come and stand at the door and wink at Urmi to console her. He would look at the pack of cards meaningfully, as if telling her, 'Come over to the office room, I will teach you a game of poker.' This was not playtime, nor was it his intention to suggest it, but he looked as if he was more mortified at the rude scolding of Urmi by her Didi. He himself could have kept her away from his work by pleading, even by mild rebuke, but it was very difficult for him to bear that Sharmila would pull Urmi up for this.

Sharmila reprimanded Shashanka also, saying, 'Why do you listen to all her whimsical biddings? She has no sense of time; it will hamper your work.'

Shashanka replied, 'Oh, come on. She is still a child. She has no companion here. How will she survive if I do not play with her sometimes?'

These were the lighter parts of life. On the other hand, when Shashanka would be seriously engaged with the plan of a building, Urmi would pull up a chair close and tell him, 'Explain it to me.' She understood it easily, the mathematical problems did not sound complex to her. Shashanka felt very happy and gave her some tasks. She did the calculations correctly. Shashanka went for supervising the work by the steam-launch of the jute company. She would demand, 'I will also go.' Not only did she accompany him, but would assist him with measurements etc., and even at times argue with him. Shashanka was delighted. This was even better than the aesthetics of perfect poetry. Hence, he would not think twice before bringing the work of chamber at home these days, for now he had an assistant for drawing a chart or calculating a sum. With Urmi by his side the work progressed well. The pace of progress might not be very fast, but the duration of time spent together seemed significant.

This is what particularly annoyed Sharmila. She could understand Urmi's childishness; she even affectionately tolerated her lapses in the housekeeping duties, but she did not at all like Urmi's easy proximity with Shashanka in matters of his business. This was an area where Sharmila had inevitably accepted the difference between the ability of her husband and herself. She considered it Urmi's insolence. The Gita had defined *swadharma* as everyone respecting his or her own propensity.

Being extremely restless, she once asked her, 'Tell me, Urmi, do you really like doing those diagrams, calculating those sums and tracing those patterns?'

'I really enjoy them, Didi.'

Sharmila retorted with disbelief, 'No, you don't, you only pretend to enjoy just to make him happy.'

All Sharmila's material care was directed to make Shashanka happy. If someone could make him happy through some other means, what was wrong in that? This simple logic did not strike her.

She repeatedly argued with Shashanka, 'Why do you waste time with her? This will harm your work. She is a child; how will she understand your complex problems?'

Shashanka replied, 'She does not understand any less than me.'

He thought he was making the elder sister happy with the praise of the younger one. Stupid!

When Shashanka had started giving less attention to his wife due to the pressure of work, Sharmila not only accepted it as inevitable, but felt proud of it also. This is why she had of late reduced the demand of her service-oriented mind. She would say the menfolk were royalty of sorts. They had to constantly expand the field of their difficult work, otherwise they would be lower in position than women. For, women fulfill their calling every day by their natural sweetness, by their inborn wealth of love. But man had to become successful through daily battles. In ancient times, kings used to lead expeditions to expand their kingdoms without any reason. It was not the lure of conquering new land, but to prove anew the pride of their manliness. Women should not stand in the way of manifesting that pride. Sharmila never stood in the way: she had deliberately allowed Shashanka full liberty to realise his objectives. At some point of time, she ensnared him in the net of her devoted service;

gradually she had reduced the scope of that net, although it pained her. Even now she served him enough, but from the background, invisibly.

Alas, today the fall of her husband from his *swadharma* was becoming apparent day by day. She could not see it, but sensed it all.

Just a glance at Shashanka's face and she could see his infatuation. This chit of a girl had shaken the seat of *sadhana* of this workaholic man in such a short time. Today, her husband's fall from grace pained Sharmila more than the suffering of disease.

There was no doubt that serious lapses were occurring in Shashanka's regular eating and dressing habits. It was often found that the dish he particularly liked was missing from the table. Some excuses were offered, but so long no excuses were tolerated in this house. Any inattentiveness was unpardonable, worthy of severe punishment. In such a controlled household, now these slips had become mere farces. It was a revolution of sorts. And whom to blame? Imagine Urmi sitting on a stool in the kitchen and guiding the cook as per Didi's instructions, simultaneously analysing many past incidents in the cook's life. Shashanka would make a sudden appearance and say, 'Leave all this now.'

'Why, what do you want me to do?'

'I have this half-day off, let us go to the Victoria Memorial. I will explain to you why the snob value of this building always makes me laugh.'

This great temptation would immediately entice Urmi and she would forget the responsibility at hand. Sharmila knew that the temporary absence of her sister would not make much difference in the quality of the food, yet Shashanka's comfort could have been enhanced by the soft care of a concerned heart. But what is the point of talking about comfort when it was obvious that her husband was extremely happy despite these apparent discomfitures.

It was from this thought that Sharmila felt quite upset. She would toss and turn in her sickbed and tell herself, 'Before dying, I have realised one important point. I have done everything, but could not make him happy. I thought I would see my reflection in Urmimala, but she is not me, she is a totally different girl!' Looking out of the window, she thought, 'She has not taken my place, I won't be able to take her place. There will surely be loss if I die, but everything will be void if she leaves.'

All these musings suddenly reminded her that winter was knocking at the door. The woollens needed to be taken out for sunning. At that time Urmi was playing a game of ping-pong with Shashanka. She called her in and said, 'Urmi, here are the keys. Go spread all the woollens on the roof-top.'

Urmi had just put the key in the lock, when an impatient Shashanka came and said, 'You can do this later. Still, there is a lot of time. Come and finish the game first.'

'But Didi—'

'Ok, I'll take Didi's permission'.

Of course, Didi gave permission, but at the same time heaved a deep sigh.

She called the maid-servant and told her, 'Give a puttee of cold water on my forehead.'

Although Urmi lost herself at this sudden liberty after so many days, she would still occasionally remember the hard responsibility of her life. She was not free; she was tied to her own penance. This penance had bonded her with a particular person whose writ ran large in her life. It was he who had fixed the nitty-gritty of her daily life. He had full right on her life—a fact Urmi could never deny. As long as Nirod was here, it was easy to agree, because she had a mental support. Now she had lost the spontaneous response from her mind, yet her sense of responsibility often pushed her. This torment of responsibility was further alienating her mind. As her own neglect became unforgiveable, she started indulging in more neglect. She would often try to keep herself distracted by gaiety and games with Shashanka, as if to keep her feeling of sorrow numbed with opium. Then again, suddenly one day she would shake her head and take out all her books from the trunk and bend over them. Then Shashanka's pranks would begin. He would pull all the books away from her, keep them inside the box again and sit tight upon it. Urmi protested, 'Shashankada, this is not fair. Please don't waste my time.'

Shashanka replied jovially, 'Wasting your time means wasting my time too. So, it cancels out.'

Urmi would struggle to snatch the books away for some time and then acquiesce. It did not seem that she was terribly upset by this. But the torment of the sense of responsibility would trouble her at least for five-six days, then it spent its force.

She told Shashanka, 'Shashankada, don't think that I am weak. I have taken an oath in my mind.'

'Pray, what is that?'

'After taking a degee from here, I will go to Europe for further medical studies.'

'After that?'

'After that I will build a hospital and take charge of it myself.'

'Whom else will you take charge of? That insufferable idiot called Nirod Mukherjee—?

Urmi put her hands on Shashanka's mouth and pleaded, 'Stop it. If you say such things, I will stop talking to you.'

Urmi repeatedly admonished herself, 'I have to be true to myself, true to myself.' She considered it infidelity on her part to show any lack of commitment to the relationship that her father himself had fixed with Nirod.

But the problem was that her feeling was not reciprocated from the other side. As if Urmi held on to a tree which had roots in the soil, but was devoid of sunlight. As a result, its leaves had turned dry and yellow. At times, she became impatient. She would think why this man could not even write a proper letter!

Urmi had studied in a convent school. Hence, her command over English was impeccable. Nirod was aware of it. Hence, he decided to impress her by writing in English. Perhaps things would have been easier had he written in Bengali. For, his knowledge of English was very poor. He would use a number of dictionary words and would make his sentences so involved that they would look like heavily loaded bullock-carts. Urmi was amused but stopped short of bursting into a laugh out of embarrassment. She admonished herself thinking that Bengalis would commit the typical mistakes in using English; laughing at it was akin to snobbery.

While in Calcutta, Nirod would often break into high-sounding sermons, but those had their own vainglory. You heard some, but you imagined more weighty imports. But long letters had no place for imagination; jargon-laden words would turn light in meaning; the content-deficit would be exposed by high-sounding words.

As long as Nirod was near her, Urmi got accustomed to all this. From a distance, however, she became only too conscious of this lapse in him. The man did not at all know how to laugh. His letter betrayed this trait very badly. She could not but compare him with Shashanka on this ground.

An occasion for such comparison presented itself the other day. While looking for a garment deep inside the box, she discovered a pair of incomplete woollen slippers. Memory of an incident four years ago flashed across her mind. Hemanta, her elder brother, was alive then. All of them had gone for an outing at Darjeeling. It was great fun. Shashanka and Hemanta kept everyone guessing and laughing at their pranks and banters. Urmi had newly learnt knitting from an aunt. She was knitting a pair of woollen slippers to gift Hemanta on his birthday. Shashanka used to tease her frequently about it. He would say, 'Whatever you gift your dada, it should not be footwear. The great sage Manu has said that it tantamounts to showing disrespect to a senior.'

Urmi had cast him a glance and asked innocently, 'Whom does the sage Manu think appropriate for such a gift then?'

Shashanka replied with a serio-comic face, 'The original right to such disrespect is of the brother-in-law.'

His right was not upheld. Once the knitting was complete, Urmi presented it to her dada. After a few days, Urmi received a letter from Shashanka which made her laugh out loud. That letter was still preserved in her box. She fished it out and read it again today:

'You left yesterday. Even before your memory could fade from our mind, a mini scandal broke out about you. I consider it immoral on my part to hide it from you.

'Many people must have noticed the worn-out slippers on my feet. Perhaps they had also noticed how the nails of my feet shone out from the slippers' many holes like the moon in a cloudless sky. (For the appropriateness of this metaphor you can consult Bharatchandra's *Annadamangal.* In case of any doubt, you can check out with your Didi). This morning when my office colleague Brindaban Nandy touched my feet for paying obeisance, the display of torn slippers cut me to the quick. I asked the servant, "Mahesh, whose lotus-feet are being adorned by my other new pair of slippers?" He replied hesitantly, "When you went to Darjeeling with Urmi-auntie and others, the new pair also went with you. But when you returned, only one pair came back with you, the other pair…" He could not complete the sentence out of embarrassment. I snarled, "Enough! Shut up now." There were other people around. Stealing a slipper is a mean job. But human mind is fickle, greed goads him or her to do such things. Hope merciful Almighty forgives them. However, even the disgrace of a low job is somewhat lessened if it is tempered by a display of intelligence. But one pair of slippers! *Tut tut*!

'So far, I have tried to protect the name of the thief. But the word will spread if she reacts with her usual garrulousness. You can seal the mouth of a detractor like Mahesh, if you quickly send an artistically knitted woollen slipper.

'Sending the size of my feet herewith.'

On receiving the letter, Urmi sat down to knit a woollen slipper with a smiling face, but she never completed it. At a point of time, she lost interest in wool-work. Today she decided to gift Shashanka this one pair of slipper to mark the anniversary of their Darjeeling trip. That day is not very far. Thinking all this, she sighed a deep sigh. Alas! Where had all those sunny mirthful days gone? They had flown away in the sky, riding light on wings. From now onwards, only duty-bound drab days showed up in the future.

It was 26 Falgun, the day of Holi, the festival of colours. For his heavy workload in the mofussil area, Shashanka had no time for such frivolity. Urmi had put *abeer* at the feet of her bed-ridden Didi. Then she sought out Shashanka at his desk, deeply absorbed in work. She stealthily approached him from behind and smeared his head with *abeer*. In the bargain his papers became coloured. The ink-pot contained red ink. Shashanka poured all of it on her sari. Getting hold of her by the hand, he snatched her pot of *abeer* and smeared her face with colour. A running, chasing, pushing, shouting bout ensued. Both forgot that time for bath and lunch had long passed. The joyous laughter of Urmimala was reverberating through the house. At last, being concerned about Shashanka's health, Sharmila had to send an emissary to stop this childishness.

The day passed. It was deep into the night. Beyond the flower-laden Krishnachuda branches, the full moon had risen in the bare sky. Suddenly, a waft of south wind rose and all the trees and plants of the garden began a commotion with a murmuring sound. The web of shadows beneath the trees also joined this commotion. Urmi sat silently by the window. She could not sleep, try as she did. The wave of excitement had not yet died down from her breast. Her mind was full with the fragrance of the mango-blossoms. The agony and the ecstasy that the Madhabilata creeper experienced to make the flowers bloom in the spring-time—Urmi's whole body also suffered from the same pang today. She went to the bathroom and splashed water on her head, and rubbed her body with a wet towel. She tossed and turned in bed for a long while and then drifted off in a sleep full of dreams.

She woke up with a jolt at 3 o'clock. The moon no longer shone through her window. The room was dark inside; there was a play of light and shade in the betel-nut grove outside. Urmi burst out into uncontrolled weeping. With her face drowned in the pillow, she wept uncontrollably. This weeping came from deep inside her heart; there was no meaning, no language attached to it. If one asked her, could she explain where this tide of pain in her body and mind was coming from? A tide that washed out the routine of the day and sleep of the night?

When Urmi woke up in the morning, her room was flooded bright with sunlight. She missed out the morning work-rituals. Sharmila forgave her, thinking that she might have been tired. Today, Urmi was full of regrets but did not know for what! Why did she get the feeling that she had lost a battle? She went to Sharmila and said, 'Didi, I am not of much use here, I might as well go back home if you agree.'

Today, Sharmila also could not say, 'No, don't go.' Rather she said, 'Ok, you may go. Your study is suffering. Come and check out with me whenever you find time.'

Shashanka had left for work. Urmi took this opportunity and immediately left for home.

Shashanka returned home with a set of instruments for mechanical drawing. He had promised Urmi to teach this art. When he did not find her at her usual spots, he came to Sharmila's room and asked, 'Where is Urmi?'

Sharmila replied, 'Her study was suffering here. So, she has gone back home.'

Shashanka sharply asked, 'She came here prepared for this disruption in study for some time. Why did she suddenly realise her difficulty today?'

From his tone, Sharmila realised that Shashanka was suspecting her role in it. Instead of getting into futile argument, she replied, 'You can bring her back, citing my preference. Hope she will not object.'

Returning home, Urmi found that Nirod's letter had come from England after a long interval. She was afraid to open it. She knew that a lot of unpardonable lapses on her part had accumulated. As an excuse for breaking the routine, she had earlier mentioned Sharmila's illness. This excuse had become untenable for some time now. Shashanka had insisted on engaging two nurses for looking after Sharmila twenty-four hours. As advised by the doctor, they restricted the free entry of relatives in the patient's room. Urmi knew in her mind that Nirod would not attach much importance to the excuse of Didi's illness. He would say, 'It is no big deal.' In fact, it was no big deal. For, she was not needed. With a repentant mind, she decided, 'I would confess and beg his pardon this time. I would promise never to commit this mistake again, never to break the regimen of studies.'

Before opening the letter, she brought out that photograph once again and put it on the table. She knew that Shashanka would tease her if he saw the photograph. Yet, Urmi would not be defensive at his barbs. This would be her way of expiating the sin. She used to gloss over the topic of her future marriage with Nirod. No one raised it either; because that topic was rather undesirable to everybody in that house. Today Urmi decided with closed fist that henceforth she would emphatically announce this news in all her daily intercourses. She had kept her engagement ring hidden for some days. Now she took it out and wore it. It was a rather cheap ring. Nirod had projected its value higher than a diamond ring with the pride of his honest poverty. The posture was like, 'It is not the ring that determines my worth, it is my worth that determines the ring's value.'

Thus purging herself sufficiently, Urmi slowly opened the letter. Reading it she jumped in joy. She felt like dancing, but she was not adept in it. The sitar was lying on the bed. She picked it up and without caring to tune it, started playing at random with bold strokes, producing loud jingling sound.

Exactly at that moment Shashanka entered the room and asked, 'What's the matter? Has the date of marriage been fixed?'

'Yes, Shashankada, it's fixed.'

'No possibility of any change?'

'No way.'

'Then shall I go ahead and book the *sehnai* player? And order *sandesh* from Bhimnag's shop?'

'You don't have to do anything.'

'So, you'll do everything yourself? Hail the heroine! And what about blessing the bride?'

'That 'bless me' amount has gone from my own pocket.'

'Frying the fish in its own fat? The riddle mystifies me.'

'Well, read this and the mystery will be clear.'

She handed over the letter to Shashanka, reading which he burst out into laughter. The letter said: the difficult research in which Nirod wanted to dedicate his life was not possible in India. So, he had to make another big sacrifice in his life. There was no other way but to sever his promised matrimonial bond with Urmi. A European lady had consented to marry him and devote her life to his cause. The work remained the same whether it was accomplished in India or England. Rajarambabu had offered to pay a sum for his research work. If a part of that sum was utilised in England, it would be showing proper respect to a departed soul. There was no impropriety in it.

Shashanka said, 'It is not a bad idea to keep the living soul alive there by occasionally doling out some money. If the supply of fund is stopped, he may become desperate out of hunger and rush back here. Keep that apprehension in mind.'

Urmi smiled and said, 'If you apprehend that, you may supply the money. I am not going to pay a penny.'

Shashanka teased, 'Hope the sulking lover will not change her mind again. Will the resolution of the fickle mind remain firm?'

'If it changes, how does it matter to you, Shashankada?'

'An honest reply will increase your vanity. So, for your own well-being I reserve my response. But, frankly, look at the cheek of the man!'

A huge burden was unloaded from Urmi's mind—a long pressing burden.

She was overwhelmed with the joy of freedom. First she tore away that self-imposed list of work. A beggar was seeking alms in the lane, she threw the engagement ring towards him.

She saked, 'Will any vendor buy the big fat books marked with pencil?'

'Even if no one does, what is the harm in their being here?'

'If the ghost of my past takes shelter in their leaves, it might reappear and stand near my bed at midnight with its index finger pointing at me.'

'If you have such fear, we won't wait for a vendor. I myself will buy out all of them.'

'What will you do with them?'

'Will cremate them following Hindu funeral rituals. I am ready to go to Gaya for performing *shradh* ceremony if that consoles your mind.'

'No, no, that would be overdoing things.'

'In that case, I would build a pyramid at the corner of my library and keep them as mummy.'

'Today, you are forbidden to go out for work.'

'The whole day?'

'Yes, the whole day.'

'What am I supposed to do?'

'We will drive out and get lost.'

'Ok, then go and get your Didi's permission.'

'No, will tell Didi on return. She would scold me, but I would rather bear it.'

'All right. I am also ready to digest the tongue-lashing of your Didi. I won't mind if we have a flat tyre on the way. I have even no objection to go to jail by over-speeding and hitting a few men on the road. But promise and utter thrice that at the end of the car journey you will come back to our house.'

'I will, I will, I will.'

After finishing their long drive both of them came to Shashanka's home at Bhabanipur. But the thrill of speed did not leave their blood. All the demands of the society, all the fear and shame were totally obliterated by this speed.

For the next few days, all Shashanka's tasks became secondary. He realised within his mind that this was not proper. The loss at the workplace could turn serious. Lying on his bed at night, he worried and exaggerated such possibilities. But the next day, he would again turn wayward, like the Yaksha of *Meghaduta*. If one drinks alcohol, one needs to drink it again to get rid of the remorsc.

SHASHANKA

Some time passed. Urmi's mind started playing tricks with her. She felt a restlessness within her. It took time for her to register the real reason. She was stunned once she realised its full impact.

Urmi was always somewhat awed by Mathurdada. She would try to avoid him. That day Mathur spent the whole morning at Didi's room. As he left, Didi sent for her. Sharmila's face was hard but calm. She said, 'Do you know the result of your regular interference with his work?'

Urmi was scared. She asked, 'What happened, Didi?'

Didi said, 'Mathurdada just informed me that your brother-in-law had not been taking interest in the business for some time now. He left it to Jawaharlal who had stolen raw material from all constructions. As a result, big warehouses that we built are reporting seepage from the roof. Their cargo is getting spoilt. They did not check on the raw material because of the reputation of our company. Now, all the reputation is lost. Over and above, we have to pay heavy compensation. Mathurdada wants to quit.'

Urmi's heart skipped a beat, her face turned pale. As if in a flash of lightning she could see the hidden mystery of her mind. She realised that at a point of time her mind had become intoxicated without her knowledge and she had lost the faculty to judge good from the bad. As if, Shashanka's work was her competitor. She was always trying to win him away from his work and have him always by her side. It happened on many occasion that when Shashanka was having a bath, a messenger would reach with some urgent piece of work. Without thinking, Urmi would dismiss him saying, 'Tell him he can't meet anyone now.'

She was apprehensive that Shashanka might immediately leave after the bath if he received the message. That would mean that Urmi might lose him for the entire day. The whole dangerous scenario of her intensely passionate game became evident to her now. Immediately she fell prostrate at Urmi's feet, repeatedly saying in a choked voice, 'Throw me out of your home. Drive me out rightaway.'

Didi had firmly decided earlier that she would never forgive Urmi. But now her heart melted.

She softly patted and caressed Urmimala's head for a while and said, 'Don't worry. We will find a way out.'

Urmi sat up and said, 'Didi, why should it be your loss only. I also have money.'

Sharmila replied, 'Have you gone mad? Don't I have some resources? I have told Mathurdada not to raise an alarm on this issue. I will quietly compensate for the loss. And mind you, your brother-in-law should never get an inkling that I have learnt everything.'

'Forgive me, Didi. Please forgive me', so saying Urmi resumed knocking her head at Sharmila's feet.

Sharmila wiped her own tears and replied in a weary tone, 'Who forgives whom, sister! This world is very complicated. What you plan does not happen; you bet your life for something, but it fizzles out.'

Henceforth, Urmi would not leave Didi for a moment. She attended to all the nitty-gritty of bathing her, feeding her, helping her lie down, administering her medicines etc. She started reading books again, but that too by the side of Didi's bed. She did not trust herself anymore, nor Shashanka.

The consequences were different. Shashanka started visiting the patient quite frequently. The typical male blindness stopped him from understanding that Sharmila easily saw the reason of his restlessness and Urmi was embarrassed and abashed. Shashanka came with the temptation of a Mohanbagan football match, but failed to tempt Urmi. He underlined the advertisement of Charlie Chaplin's name in the newspaper and showed it to Urmi, but to no avail. When Urmi was not so unavailable, Shashanka used to manage his work despite all hindrances, but now he found it impossible to work.

At the beginning, Sharmila felt happy in spite of the meaningless torture of her hapless husband. But gradually she noticed that his agony was turning unbearable; his cheeks became sunken; there were dark shadows under his eyes. It was obvious from his appearance that since Urmi did not give him company during meals, he had lost interest in food. The great tide of joy that visited this house recently had totally ebbed. But the easy routine life that they earlier had also did not return.

Once upon a time Shashanka was totally indifferent to his appearance. He had his hair cut so close by the barber that there was no necessity of combing the hair. Sharmila had argued and quarrelled over it on many occasions but all in vain. Whereas Urmimala's mild admonishing with derisive laughter did not fail to evoke a response. Shashanka not only started growing long hair, but would groom it with perfumed oil. But these days his unkempt hair reflected his mental agony, to the extent that one could not openly laugh at it any more. Sharmila's anxiety overtook her anguish. Her heart ached with pity for her husband and condemnation for herself. Consequently, her poor physical condition further aggravated.

There was a parade and dress rehearsal for war at the Maidan. Shashanka asked with trepidation, 'Will you like to go, Urmi? I have reserved two premium seats.'

Before Urmi could respond, Sharmila blurted out, 'Of course, she will go. She is dying to go out for a while.'

This indulgence prompted Shashanka propose a couple of days later, 'What about a trip to the circus?'

It seemed Urmi easily enthused to this proposal.

A few days later, 'Botanical gardens?'

This she was hesitant about. She would not like to go away for long, leaving Didi behind.

But Didi herself took Shashanka's side. The man was working hard with labourers day in and day out. Without a little relaxation, his health would run down.

By the same logic, it was thought normal that they go on a steamer trip to Raiganj one evening.

Sharmila thought within herself that he would not be able bear the loss of the person herself for whom he was ready to lose his work.

Although nobody had clearly told Shashanka anything, he felt that he was receiving an unspoken support from all quarters. He had assumed that Sharmila was not particularly pained by the development and she would be happy to see them happy together. An ordinary woman would have found it impossible, but Sharmila was extraordinary. When Shashanka was still in service, an artist sketched Sharmila with a coloured pencil. It was in his folio bag so long. He took it out and got it fashionably framed in a foreign shop, and hung it on the wall in his office just opposite his chair. A flower-vase was placed beneath it and the gardener was asked to put fresh flowers in it every morning.

At last, one day while showing Urmi the sunflower blossom in the garden, Shashanka held her hand and said, 'I am sure you know that I love you, and your Didi is a goddess incarnate. I respect her more than anyone else in this world. She is out of the world, much above us.'

Didi had repeatedly impressed upon Urmi that in the event of her death her greatest satisfaction would be Urmi's presence. She would be pained to even imagine the appearance of any other woman in this household, and yet she would not be able to tolerate a situation where there would be no woman to look after Shashanka. Didi had even impressed upon her the business compulsion part: if his love was thwarted, all his work would be neglected and lost in that shock. When his mind was satiated, there would be spontaneous discipline in work.

Shashanka's mind swelled up. He was living in such an imaginary land that all the responsibilities of the work-a-day world was lost in day-dreaming. These days, his devotion to observe Sundays was like a true blue Christian. One Saturday, he told Sharmila, 'Look, I have been spared a steam launch from the European Manager of the jute mill. Thinking of taking a ride tomorrow early morning with Urmi, will go up to Diamond Harbour and return by the evening.'

Sharmila's heart sank. Her forehead showed wrinkles of agony. Shashanka did not even notice.

She feebly asked, 'What about lunch?'

Shashanka replied, 'That I have arranged with a hotel.'

There was a time when Sharmila was in control of all these arrangements. Shashanka was rather indifferent. Now things had gone in a reverse order.

The moment Sharmila uttered, 'It's all right then,' Shashanka immediately ran out of the room. Sharmila felt like crying out. Pressing her face on the pillow, she mumbled, 'Oh God, why am I still alive?'

Tomorrow Sunday was their marriage anniversary. Till date, there had been no disruption in celebrating this day. This time also, Sharmila had made all arrangements from the bed, without telling Shashanka. No lavish party; she would make Shashanka wear the red dhoti of Benaras that he wore on their marriage day, she would wear the silk sari. She would burn incense, garland her husband and feed him his favourite dishes. The *shehnai* would play on the gramophone. In other years, Shashanka used to buy her a surprise gift. Sharmila had imagined this would surely happen this year also.

Now, Sharmila was finding even these thoughts unbearable. Whenever her room was empty, she kept murmuring, 'False! False! False! What's the point in this make-believe relation?'

She could not sleep at night. At dawn, she heard the sound of the motor-car leaving their doors. Sharmila sobbed inconsolably, saying, 'Oh God, you are false!'

From this point, her health started deteriorating fast. One day when the symptoms were at their peak, Sharmila called for her husband. It was dusk. Her room was dimly lit. She gestured at the nurse to leave the room. Making him sit near her, she held Shashanka's hand and said, 'You are the boon that I got from God in this life. But He did not give me enough energy to keep the boon. I have done my best. Still, I must have committed many mistakes. Please forgive me.'

Shashanka was about to say something, but she stopped him and continued, 'No, don't say anything. I am leaving Urmi in your hands. She is my own blood. You will find me in her. You will find much more that you didn't find in me. No, please shut your lips, do not utter a word. Lady Luck smiled at me at the time of death. I could make you happy.'

Nurse declared from outside, 'Doctor has come.'

Sharmila said, 'Send him in.'

The conversation stopped.

***

Sharmila had a maternal uncle who was much in favour of alternative medicine. Of late, he was devoted to a sannyasi who had come down from the Himalayas. When the doctors virtually gave up on Sharmila, he insisted that the herbal medicine of the sannyasi *babaji* must be tried. The powdered root of a Tibetan plant and a large quantity of milk—these were the ingredients of the medicine.

Shashanka had an instinctive dislike for quacks. He objected to any such treatment. Sharmila pleaded, 'Nothing is of any use any more. But at least Mama will have his consolation.'

Surprisingly, the medicine started working. The breathing trouble subsided, the blood vomiting ceased.

After a fortnight, Sharmila sat up on the bed. The doctor said that sometimes pushed to the brink by imminent death, the body draws on its reserve energy and heals itself.

Sharmila survived. But she thought, 'What do I do now? This survival may turn worse than death for me.'

Urmi was packing her bags. Her innings here had come to an end.

Sharmila told her, 'You can't leave.'

'What nonsense!'

'Have not you heard of instances in a Hindu family where two sisters live like co-wives?'

'Shame on you!'

'Afraid of scandal? Is the neighbour's gossip more important than God's decree?'

She called Shashanka and proposed, 'Let us go away to Nepal. Was not the royal court bent on hiring you? There will be no scandal in a new country.'

Sharmila did not allow anyone any opportunity to raise objection. The arrangement for their voyage to Nepal was going on in full swing. Yet, Urmi often hid herself in corners and moved around with a sad and confused expression.

Shashanka told her, 'Think of what will happen to me if you leave me today.'

Urmi replied, 'I can't think any more. Whatever you two decide is all right with me.'

It took a few days to make arrangements for the trip. When the day of journey was approaching, Urmi said, 'Give me a week's time. I would go to my place and organise things with Manager Kaka.'

After Urmi left, Mathur came to Sharmila with a grave expression. He said, 'You are leaving at the right time. After my last discussion with you, I divided work for Shashanka on a separate plank. I released him from all obligations of loss or gain with my affairs. Recently, Shashanka was winding up all pending work and settling the account. Thus it came to light that all your money has gone astray. Even beyond that, the burden of debt is so heavy that perhaps the house will have to be sold.'

Sharmila asked, 'How come the extent of damage was so huge and yet he did not even get wind of it?'

Mathur replied, 'The misfortune is like a thunderbolt. It does not let you know even moments before it hits. He was aware that he was incurring loses. Things could have been controlled at that point. But misfortune is often fraught with mischievous thoughts. To quickly repair the loopholes of the business, he engaged in the game of speculation in the coal market. All without my knowledge. But in that too, a point came when he had to sell cheap what he had bought at a premium. Suddenly he found that everything he had, had vanished like a rocket; only the ash remained. Now, if he gets a job in Nepal by the grace of God, you all will be saved.'

Sharmila was not afraid of poverty. On the contrary, she knew that her position in the household would be further elevated in the days of penury. She was confident that she could lighten the sting of poverty by her deft handling of things. Moreover, her ornaments would easily see them through for quite a while. And in spite of herself she could not help think that if Shashanka married Urmi, her property too would belong to him. But it was not enough just to live comfortably. What hurt her more was the ignominy of the fact that the wealth her husband created by virtue of his own intelligence and hard work and for which Sharmila made many sacrifices was all gone today. Their combined hope and aspiration had vanished like a mirage. She thought, if I had died, I would have at least been spared this downfall. Now, I would suffer my destiny, but would not this life in penury one day bring terrible remorse in Shashanka's mind? He might not be able to forgive Urmi, infatuation with whom had led him to neglect his business. At that time, the food served by her would taste like poison for him. He would be ashamed of the result of his drunkenness, but would blame the drink for it. If at last it became imperative to depend on Urmi's property, the indignation resulting out of loss of self-respect would drive him to treat Urmi with biting sarcasm and contempt.

On the other hand, while running through the balance sheet with Mathur, Shashanka suddenly discovered that all Sharmila's money had sunk in his business. She had not told him anything, but quietly settled it with Mathur.

Shashanka remembered that after resigning from his job he built up his business with Sharmila's money. Today, closing a lost business, he was going for a job with the burden of Sharmila's debt on his head, a debt he may not be able to repay in his lifetime.

Another ten days to start for Nepal; Shashanka could not sleep through the night. At dawn, he jumped out of the bed and standing in front of the mirror, he banged his fists on the table, saying, 'I am not going to Nepal.' He took a firm decision, 'Both of us will live with Urmi right here, in this city of Calcutta, ignoring the frowning of disapproval of the society. And I would rebuild my fragile business again, in this city of Calcutta.'

Sharmila was making a list of the items that they would carry along and the items they would leave behind. Suddenly she heard Shashanka calling, 'Sharmila! Sharmila!' Leaving the lists behind, she rushed to her husband's room. In anticipation of more bad news, she asked with a lot of trepidation, 'What happened?'

Shashanka declared, 'We shall not go to Nepal. We shall not care for the society. We will stay here.'

Sharmila asked, 'But why? What happened?'

Shashanka said, 'I have work to do.'

That old dialogue—I have work to do. Sharmila's heart trembled.

'Sharmi, don't think that I am a coward. Can you even imagine such degradation in me that I would run away from my duty?'

Sharmila went near him and took his hands in hers. She said, 'Tell me in clear terms what you have in mind.'

Shashanka said, 'Please do not try to suppress the fact that I have again taken loan from you.'

Sharmila said, 'All right. You have. So?'

Shashanka replied, 'Like old times, here I am again, starting work to repay the loan. Mark my word, I will win back whatever I have lost. Have faith in me again like once you trusted me.'

Sharmila rested her head on her husband's chest and said, 'You also have trust in me. Teach me how to work; from today onwards mould me as your worthy companion.'

The peon called from outside, 'Letter! Letter!'

There were two letters written by Urmi. One was addressed to Shashanka—

I am now on way to Bombay. From there to England. Will return as a doctor as ordained by Father. It would take six-seven years. Whatever damage I have done at your home will be repaired by Time in the meanwhile. Do not worry for me; I will worry for you, though.

To Sharmila—

Didi, I bow at your feet. Please forgive the sin I have committed unknowingly. I will be happy to know from you that it was not a sin. Will not nurture the desire for any more happiness. In fact, do I even know for sure what gives me happiness? It does not matter if happiness eludes me. What I fear is committing futher mistake.

GLOSSARY

Veena: An Indian stringed instrument, with four main and three auxiliary strings. The southern type has a lute-like body; the older northern type has a tubular body and a gourd fitted to each end as a resonator.

Gamchha: It is a traditional thin, coarse, cotton towel found in India, Bangladesh, as well as various parts of South and Southeast Asia and is used to dry the body after bathing or wiping sweat. It is often just worn on one side of the shoulder. Its appearance varies from region to region, and it has also been traditionally worn as a scarf. The gamucha is most commonly found with checks and striped patterns of red, orange or green. Plain white gamchhas with coloured (embroidered or printed) borders from Odisha and Assam are local handicrafts, and may be worn around the neck with traditional Indian attire.

Kakababu: Uncle; father's younger brother or even younger male cousin

Pakhawaj: The *pakhawaj* or *mridang* is an Indian barrel-shaped, two-headed drum, a variant and descendant of the older *mridang*. It is the standard percussion instrument for the dhrupad style of music and also for classical dance. It has a low, mellow tone, very rich in harmonics. The *pakhawaj* is played mostly by hitting the full palm on the surface and not the finger tips as in the tabla.

Kalapahad: Kalapahad was the title of Rajiv Lochan Ray or Kalachand Roy Bhadury a Bengali (Barendra Brahmin) general of Gour Sultanate, who converted to Islam after falling in love with and marrying the daughter of an Afghan governor in Bengal, Sulaiman Karrani. After conversion to Islam, Roy became Muhammad Farmuli, but is popularly known as *Kalapahad* or the 'Black Mountain', the destroyer. He is fabled to have been instrumental in conquering parts of Odisha for the Afghans of Bengal, and destroying ancient sculpture and temples in 1538.

Juju: An imaginary ghostly character in folklore and myths, the juju is often evoked by the mothers of very young children while putting them to sleep, as a fearsome entity lurking in dark corners and ready to pounce.

Abhimaan: The subtle emotions of the broken-hearted lover or spouse, which are often not spelt out but quietly nursed in the heart. It is a word to describe a degree of upset/grudge one holds against a loved one or someone one is close to. It is a 'softer' form of anger, disappointment or hurt.

Sadhana: Disciplined or dedicated practice or learning, especially in religion or music.

Abeer: Powdered colours, popularly called *phaag* or *rangoli* in the rest of India, the abeer in Bengal is used to play and smear friends and family with dry colours on the day of Holi. Historically it is also linked to the Radha-Krishna saga and is a symbol of their romance.

Krishnachuda: Krishnachuda (*Delonix regia*) in West Bengal, Odisha and Assam, it is commonly known as the Gulmohar or the Mayflower tree in India. It is widely found all across the world and is loved for its beautiful flaming red canopy in the flowering season, which is spring in India.

Madhabilata: *Hiptage benghalensis*, often simply called hiptage, is a perennial, evergreen liana native to India, Southeast Asia and the Philippines. Its habitat is variable and prefers climates ranging from warm temperate to tropical. It is also referred to as Madhoilata.

Shehnai: The shehnai is a musical instrument, common in India, Pakistan and Bangladesh. It is made out of wood, with a double reed at one end and a metal or wooden flared bell at the other end. Its sound is thought to create and maintain a sense of auspiciousness and sanctity and, as a result, is widely used during marriages, processions and in temples although it is also played in concerts. The *shehnai* is similar to South India's *nadaswaram*.

Sandesh: A very popular sweet (dessert) native to Bengal, particularly to Kolkata. Made of fresh cottage cheese (made by curdling milk). It is a Bengali delicacy, called '*praanahara*' in present Bangladesh. Sometimes jaggery or dry fruits are added to it. It is a popular item at Bengali wedding feasts and other celebratory social events.